This book belongs to my friend

BOYD-FRIEND

written by PATRICIA WATKINS

FRAYED PAGES PUBLISHING · FRAYED PAGES PUBLISHING · UNITED STATES OF AMERICA

FRAYED
PAGES
PUBLISHING

Published in Pickens, South Carolina, United States of America

Information and requests for special purchases and promotional sales may be addressed to ~~BHB International, Inc.~~ THE AUTHOR
~~302 West North 2nd Street, Seneca, SC 29678~~
~~864 885 9411 · Email bhbintl@bellsouth.net~~

Printed in the United States of America

Library of Congress Control Number: 2004093481

ISBN 0-9753397-0-2

A portion of the sales from this book
will be given to animal organizations that are devoted
to rescuing, fostering and re-homing healthy, adoptable animals.

Whenever, wherever, however possible,
please consider taking an active part to help animals in your community.

It's true...
there is a time for everything
and a season for every activity under heaven...
even for the welfare of our animals.

And...
it is my hope
that after reading this book
for simple pleasure
or
for the joy of learning,
you might someday have
your own four-legged friend,
mindful of the saying...

A friend loves at all times.

May your life be filled with Boyd-Friends.

CHAPTER ONE
WHERE AM I?

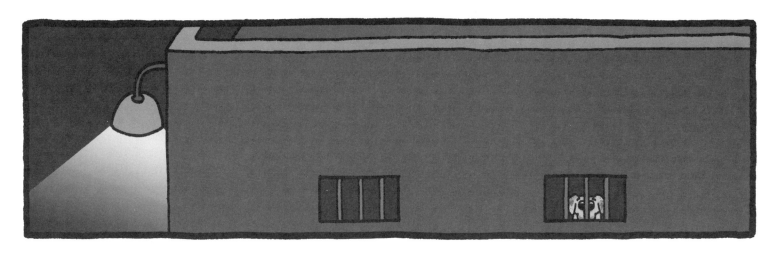

Oh me, oh my... why is it taking Elaine sooooo long?
I overheard her talking to one of the workers.
She said she was going to email one more friend a plea for my adoption.
Isn't that exciting news?
I hope her friend will understand my needs.
You see... I have great expectations!

"Hey, keep it down over there!" bark the large dogs in my section of the shelter.

I will try not to bark because if I awaken the others they will be grizzly!
So I'll be quiet as a mouse and whisper my story to you.
Shhh... be still and we will not disturb them.
I'll tell you all that I remember before dawn.
The other dogs are so loud in the morning that I cannot hear my own bark!
Well... cough, cough... that is, if I could bark.
I'm so weak that I do not even want to try.
But I'll be warm if I lean against these softer dogs beside me.
Hmmm... I wonder how my bony legs came to have so many hairless spots.
I really don't remember how the big men caught me.
Oh me, oh my... I was running sooo fast!
I was not running away from anything or anyone.
Oh, my goodness, no! I was hungry and lonely.
I had no food and I had no one to help me.
You see... I was running to find a friend.

Anyway, as I remember, I came from a back porch.
It was not at all cozy. But I did like hearing the indoor sounds and smelling the food.
And I would always eat when the house people remembered to feed me.

I thought they would feed me before they left.
They walked by me many times with furniture.
In and out, in and out they walked for hours.
But I was playing with the empty boxes.
So I suppose they didn't see me.

I waited and waited for the house people to return. I really thought they would.
In the past they always came back, even if it was a whole weekend.
But this time was different. They were gone for a very long time.
Day after day after day I waited for them on the porch.
I was fortunate to have drinking water because it rained a lot.
But after four days without food my tummy was very hungry.

I ran down the street to see if I could find something to eat.
I heard slamming doors and people yelling at me from their windows.
There was no mistake that my nose was guiding me to food.
Great cooking smells from their homes were beginning to make me feel better already!
But somehow there was not enough for me.
I discovered that most house people were too busy for me.
They wanted me out of their yard and out of their sight.
They said I didn't look like any special kind of dog.
I was embarrassed when they pointed to my spotty hair and bony sides.
I showed my friendly smile. But I was told that my teeth were anything but white.
People pointed to my ribs and said I had that yucky-doggie odor.
House people would not touch me and did not allow little people to come near me.
How would I ever have a friend?

My hungry tummy would not let me rest.
So I ran down another street looking for food.
I ran down the next street faster.
Then I ran faster and faster.
Suddenly I did not know where I was.
I didn't know where to go and no one knew my name.
The daylight was disappearing so I ran with all my might.
Then, well... I don't remember what happened.

When I opened my eyes I was in a big truck full of cages with barking dogs.
The men in front were yelling, "Quiet! No more barking!"
But we didn't know who they were. We had never seen them before.

I felt very nervous and afraid. Why was I in a cage? Where was I going?
The damp air in the truck was making me feel sick.
It was a bumpy ride and I slid from side to side in my cage for hours.
All I could think about was food and finding a friend.

Suddenly the truck stopped and all was quiet.
We heard approaching footsteps and faint barking sounds.
The back doors of the truck opened wide and we saw a man and a woman.
They helped us out and brought us into this building.
We were found! How great was that?

The woman pulled me from my cage.
I could tell she liked me because she was giving me a collar!
I didn't mind that it was a little tight around my neck.
Heck, I never had one of my own and this one had a number!
I was number 144!
There was a lot of talk about where to put me.
I was too large for the small, clean cages in the front of the shelter.
And I was too small and fragile to put with the big ones in the middle.
I heard the woman tell the man to put me into number 22.
She said the other dogs might help break the chill of the concrete and keep me warm.
That was thoughtful. Wasn't it?
She might like to be my friend.

Then the best thing happened.
A man gave me a big bowl of dry food!
I ate it so dog-gone fast that he filled it again and two more times!
Oh me, oh my... I ate as much as four dogs!

At least that's what he said before he placed me in this kennel.
And 'Ta-Dum'... here I am! That's how I came to be in this animal shelter.
Anyway, who would have believed that all seven of us would fit in this tiny space?
The woman was right. We do stay warm when we huddle together.
Yawn...cough, cough. Oh me, oh my... I still remember that big meal!
It's a good thing I ate so much when I arrived.
Because now I get pushed away from my bowl before I have a chance to finish.
I don't think the others are rude. I think they are hungry like I was when I arrived.

Oh well, I always have water.
It doesn't taste like rainwater. It has an odor, but I don't mind.
At least I am not alone any more.
Still, somehow being here is not exactly like having a friend.
I mean, gee, I would like to meet all the people in this shelter.
But that will not be easy because they do not all come back this far.
They don't have time.
There are so few people who work here and so many of us.

I'll close my sleepy eyes for now and dream of having a friend.
It is my dream that someday all of us will have a friend.
Someone will love us. I just know it! And we will love them forever!
Someday it will happen. Just you wait and see! I believe that with all my heart!
We'll always be there for each other because friends always... alwayzzzzzzz...

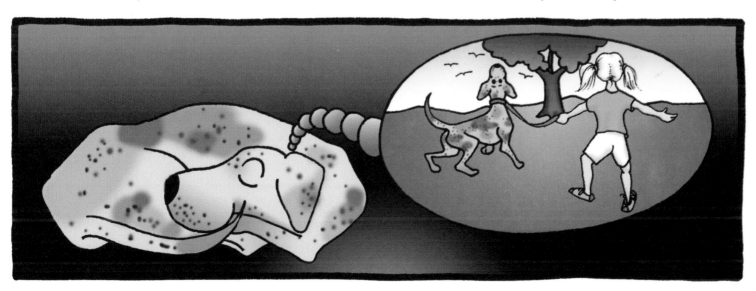

Oh me, oh my... this must be a special morning.
Someone is coming through the swinging doors.
Wow! It's great to see someone this early!
Who? Me?
You came for me?
What operation?
Elaine didn't tell me about an operation.
Do you think I am strong enough?
Maybe we should wait another day or two...

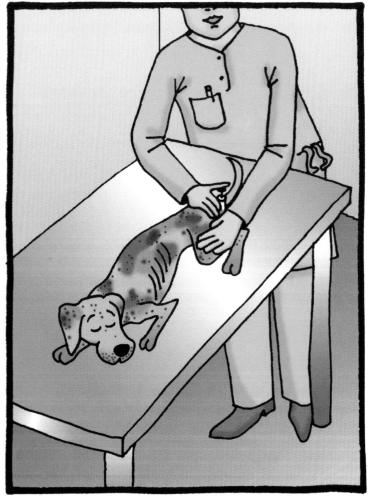

Wow! This room is very warm and bright!
And everything smells so clean.

But I'm feeling tired and sleepy now.
So I think I'll take a little nap right here.

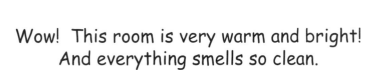

10

Hey, back off! Okay?
It's me, but I'm sleepy and sore.
I don't know where I picked up this smell.
But it's really me! Back off!
I just need to sit. Oops... no sitting!
I'll just curl in this little corner.
Don't ask me where I was. I don't know.
And I have no idea what happened.
Oh, go ahead. Take all my food!
I don't feel like eating anything today.
I just want to sleep.

How can it be dark again?
Did I sleep all day?
Okay, okay... I'm huddling!
Hey, buster... watch it!
My whole body aches.
Do I look as sleepy as I feel?
Ouch! Go find another side for a pillow!
This is my space for the night and I'm sticking to it!

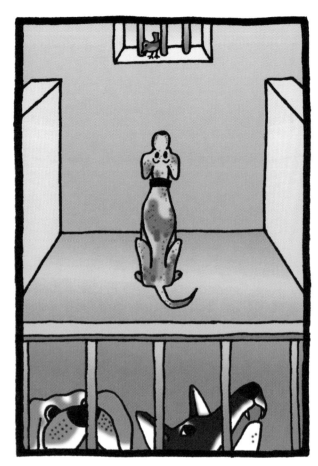

Okay, okay! I'm awake already! Don't be so pushy!
Hmmm... I remember a shiny table somewhere.

Hey, I do feel a little better today.
I think I'm back in the saddle again.
Ouch! I can't believe I had that thought!

Of course I want to eat today!
Oh me, oh my... another day, another holler.
I wish this day could begin without barking.

What? Me again?
Oh, no! Not again!
You must be mistaken. Not me!
Surely you want someone else.
No, please! Don't pick me up.
I'll walk... thank you very much.
Use the leash, please.
It's easier. Trust me on this one.

What?
I'm going to meet Elaine's friend?
Really? Oh me, oh my...
YIPPIE-SKIPPIE and JUMPIN' JACKRABBITS!
Hey, everybody... I'm going to meet a friend!
A friend! Oh, wow! Are you sure?
I have dreamed about a friend all my life!
Could this be my dream-come-true day?
I sure hope the friend likes me!

I'm so excited that I cannot walk straight!
Oh, a friend! A friend! I'm going to meet a friend!
One more hallway and one more turn...
Look out, friend... here I come!

Gasp! There's Elaine!
And that must be the friend beside her.

Do you know what makes a friend so special?
Well, the very fact they come to visit you, of course!
And it looks like the friend is happy to see me!

13

Chapter 2
WHO AM I?

Can you believe I am here with Elaine's friend?
This is a very happy moment for me!

"Oh, he's wonderful," says the friend. "He's so timid and sweet.
But, oh me, oh my... he's so frail. Is he really eighteen months old?"

What? What did I hear? What did you say?
That 'oh me, oh my' thing. That's my line!
This friend speaks my language!
YIPPIE-SKIPPIE! How about that?
This is more than I ever could have dreamed!
Hey... I'm not dreaming. Am I?

Yikes! This might be trouble.
Elaine is showing the friend my records.

"You're fortunate. He is worm-free."

Now hold on just a minute.
I'm the favored one here.
I'm the one without worms!
What if this friend has worms?
Then what would I do? Huh?
Did you ever think of that?
Well, did you?

The friend seems happy that I am current with all my vaccines.
She smiles and asks if I have that kennel cough thing.
Oh, no! She had to say the words 'kennel cough.'
Whenever I hear those words, I feel like coughing.
She probably won't want me now.

15

What? She doesn't mind? Someone scratch me!
The friend says she has cared for lots of animals.
She says that she will help my cough thing heal soon.
And that's not all. I'm going to meet her veterinarian next week!

"I love you, little guy," she says. "You leave your cares behind.
It's time for you to get healthy!
No more nasty cough and no more running about for you!"

How did she know I ran for my life?
YIPPIE-SKIPPIE! Look at this!
A new collar and leash!
Oh me, oh my! My favorite colors!
Well, I can't actually see color.
But it sure looks great to me!
I'll take it! Wow! It's a perfect fit!
Wait until the guys in my cage see me now!

What? A truck? We're going for a truck ride?
But, what about showing my new collar to my huddle-buddies?
Okay, maybe some other time.

Are you kidding?
We're going to share this entire front seat?
I have dreamed of riding in a truck someday!
Whoa! Is this really happening?

"Hey, boy. It's okay. You'll be well soon. I promise.
Boy... hey, there... hey, boy!
Well, look at that! You like the sound of boy!
Okay, your name will be Boyd... Boyd-Friend.
I think more than anything in the world you need a friend.
I will be your forever friend no matter where you live.

Soon your sickness will be gone and you will be healthy.
Then we'll have great fun!
We'll learn words, play games and laugh at each other.
But most important of all, you will be loved.
Shhh... be quiet now and rest while I drive."

17

"Look, Boyd-Friend! We're here!
Easy, easy little guy.
Let's put on your leash and take a short walk.
There you go... outside.
That's a good Boyd!"

Wow! This is my kind of place!
Lots and lots of trees!
Trees for well, you know... for shade, of course.

Whoa! Now this is a fence!
But I think I can wiggle through right here... oops!
It's too strong to go through.
It's too sturdy to crawl under.
And it's much too high to climb.
Are fences built for keeping things in?
Or are they built for keeping things out?
Anyway, I have no reason to leave.
I'll go exploring!

Gee, what a nice barn.
It smells fresh and clean and it even has running water and painted floors!
Oh me, oh my... would you look at that kennel!
I can only imagine sleeping on something so soft.
Someone must be very special to sleep in there with all those toys!

What? It's for me? Really? This sleeping place is a dream come true!
Just listen to that beautiful music! Is this place perfect or what?
I'll just curl on this blanket. Yawn... it's so nice and fuzzzzzzzzzzzzy.

"Have a good nap, Boyd-Friend. I'll be back in about three hours."

Hello, friend!
Has it really been three hours?
Sure! I'll go for a walk!

Whew! Exercising is fun!
But it sure makes me tired.
Now I'm ready for more sleep.
I can hardly hold my eyes open.

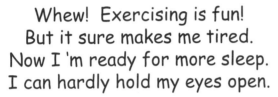

Hello again! I sure am hungry!
I was just dreaming of something to eat!
Ummm... yummy!
And now it's time for another walk?
Hey, I'm liking this routine thing!

Not a problem... I would love to go back to my warm kennel.
I like falling asleep with these soft melodies.
And the night light... only a friend would think of such a thing!
Thank you, friend. I love you, friend.
I'll just cuddle in my blanket. It's so cozzzzzzzzzzy...

20

Hey, there! It's morning already?
You didn't leave me. You're still here!
No one has ever given me clean bedding.
Where did you learn to be such a wonderful friend?

I've been resting in this cozy barn for ten days.
And this morning I feel different.
Yes, I feel stronger! I feel more alive!
That's it! I can breathe easier!
Wow! I'm not coughing any more!
I have more energy! I really am getting well!
My friend was right... she kept her word.
I am getting healthy!
JUMPIN' JACKRABBITS!

21

Look at me! I am able to walk a little better now.
I think I'll look around and see what's in here.
Hmmm... a table, some chairs, a sink, a stove, an Oven Puppy.
What? An Oven Puppy? I can't believe my eyes!
Look at the puppy in this oven! See, right here!
Look right here in this glass oven door. See?

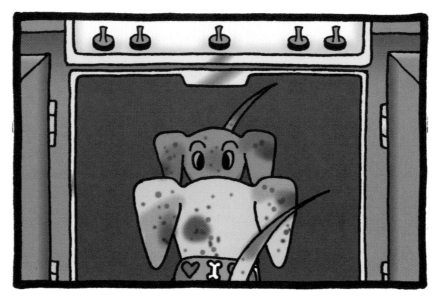

YIPPIE-SKIPPIE! Would you look at this!
It sure is an Oven Puppy! How about that?
I have another new friend... Oven Puppy!
Oh, Oven Puppy. I could stand here all day and look at you!
I like your soft eyes and perky ears.
And just look at you wag that tail!
You're about my size and you have freckles and spots just like me!
I love you, Oven Puppy! Don't ever go away!
Uh-oh... I have to go outside.
My friend says I still need lots of walking and fresh air.
You stay right there, Oven Puppy.

"Whoa! Slow down, Boyd-Friend.
You're walking with a new spring in your step today!
Let's walk by the water bowl and see if you need a drink.
That's a good Boyd. Have a nice, long drink."

What! Look at this!
I can't believe my eyes! Am I dreaming?
No. I'm not dreaming. I'm wide awake!
Look! Look in this shiny bowl.
It's another new friend... Bowl Puppy!
Can you believe I have so many new friends?
Hello, Bowl Puppy! You are the funniest!
You look a lot like my friend, Oven Puppy.
Do you like to blow bubbles in the water like I do?
JUMPIN' JACKRABBITS!
You're fun to play with in the water!
Look at you! You pop up all around the bowl!
You're really fast, Bowl Puppy!

"Come along, Boyd-Friend.
You need some walking before your bath.
Only clean dogs may come into my home.
And you are healthy enough for a bath this afternoon."

Excuse me. Did you say home?
Home with you? I'm not going back to the barn?
Hey, suds me up and hose me down!
Make me look like a funny clown!

A bath is a small price to pay to stay in a home!
At least, I think it is. I've never been inside a home before.
I wonder what I will find. Oh me, oh my... I'm really excited!

Can you believe that my friend is sharing her home with me?
She must love me very, very much. How should I behave?
I must remember that carpet and rugs are not grass!
I'll be careful not to break things and I promise not to beg for food.
I don't beg any more. My friend always remembers to feed me.

Ahhh... here I go right through the front door!
Can you believe this? Just look at this space! There are so many things to see.

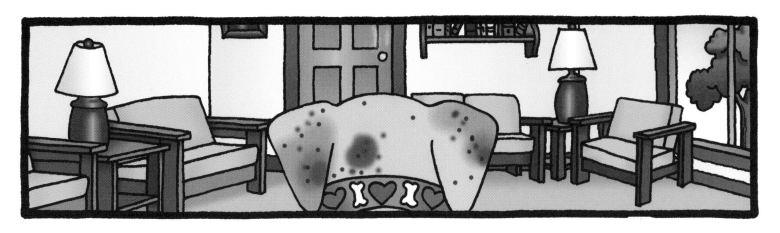

Why, I could just... what?
Well, hello there! How very nice to meet you, too!
Yes, yes! I see you, Lamp Puppy!

"My goodness, Boyd Friend!
You have discovered yourself in that shiny lamp!"

You make me smile, Lamp Puppy!
I did not know you lived here!
I will be back to play with you later.
I'm taking the house tour right now.

"Okay, Boyd-Friend, come this way.
This is the kitchen, a room you will likely enjoy.
And, of course, this is the famous treat jar.
It's famous because it is never empty!"

Well, would you look at that! Who would have thought?
Imagine finding you here on the counter!
Hello, Mixer Puppy! My name is Boyd-Friend.
I see you have a friend too! Hello, Teapot Puppy!

"Look at you, Boyd-Friend! Yes, that is you!
You are amazing how you see yourself in shiny objects.
Let's move back and let me into the cupboard.
We need to use a large cooking pan for preparing dinner.
You can be the master food taster as we make our soup!"

Hey, wait! Look! It's a Pan Puppy...lots of Pan Puppies!
You are the most handsome Pan Puppies I have ever seen!
I think we will see each other often in this room.
Yummm... smell those muffins!
I remember smelling those when I was resting in the barn.
Yep, that fresh-baked treat smell drifted right down to my kennel.
That is how I know this is a good place to eat!

26

"Let's gather some small towels before we begin cooking.
This is the laundry room, Boyd-Friend.
And depending on your manners, it may be your bedroom."

Gasp! Oh, no! Can this be happening?
I'm looking at the most beautiful puppy in the world!
You are magnificent, Washer Puppy!
And I am the most fortunate dog in the world!
Hello, Washer Puppy! I'm Boyd-Friend!
Isn't it unusual that we look so much alike?
Hey, you wiggle and wink just like me!
Do you know Oven Puppy?
You sure look a lot like him!
Maybe someday we can all play together.
After all, we are friends!

"There you are, Mr. Reflection.
Here... try this piece of carrot.
That's yummy, isn't it?
How about broccoli? Ohhh... you like that!
I have never had a rescue that didn't like broccoli.
You all seem to like the crunch.
Someday we will tell your forever family all about you.
We'll tell them about your favorite fresh foods.
And everyone will chuckle about your reflection games!"

Wait a minute. What rescue?
I'm not Rescue.
I am Boyd-Friend. Remember?

27

Chapter 3
I AM LOVED!

Now I am really confused!
Am I a rescue?
But I thought I was showing good behavior.
I'm not going anywhere. This is my home.
Home is where your reflection is. Right?
I'm going to speak with my friend, Washer Puppy.
Maybe he will help me understand.

"Hello. Yes, I am Boyd-Friend's foster mother.
Oh, I remember. Our neighbor, Becky, told you.
Yes... on the Internet. He is a darling!
We have received many emails and calls.
Well, no decision has been made yet.
Sure. I would be happy to read your application."

Do you want to know something, Washer Puppy?
I remember being in a big building.
And I had to huddle with other dogs to stay warm.
I was very sick... always coughing.
Then I left that place and came here.
Does that make me a rescue?

"Absolutely. All records are given to the owners.
Yes, spay and neuter help to reduce the problem of over-population.
It even gives them a better chance for a healthier, long life."

So that was my operation! I'll be dogged!

"Well, every animal and every adoption is different.
And it's hard to refuse help to such gentle souls.
I so enjoy their character just waiting to be discovered."

How about that? I'm gentle! I have character!
These spots on me are not just funny markings.
They are characters! Wow!
I have five shades of characters!
And all my characters are waiting to be noticed.
But, wait... I thought I was found. Wasn't I?

"We bring them home and love them to health.
Yes, whatever it takes for their recovery.
We constantly work on behavior, obedience and socializing."

YIPPIE-SKIPPIE! I have become healthy!
I really like having yummy food in my tummy.
My favorite is turkey and broth.
Of course, I do like almost all raw veggies.
Do you have favorite foods, Washer Puppy?
Oh me, oh my... dessert is to drool for... and I always do!
I'll do just about anything for yogurt or blueberries.
Have you ever had a mouth full of frozen blueberries?
They are the best... chilly tongue and all!
And isn't it funny how we get belly rubs after dessert?
Sometimes it is the smallest things that amuse people.

"Well, actually, the length of time varies.
But a lot of work still remains for the adopting family.
Yes, a responsible child and younger sister might be good.
Let's see if Sara is interested in the duties of pet ownership.
She could teach little Anna by example as she cares for Boyd.
Oh, tomorrow morning about ten o'clock would be fine.
Okay, we'll see you then."

"Time for bed, Boyd-Friend.
You have a busy day ahead of you tomorrow.
Have a good night's rest.
I'll see you in the morning."

Good morning, Lamp Puppy!
It's going to be a busy day! Do you know what busy is?
I think it means there are many things to do.
I think I am going to like this kind of day!

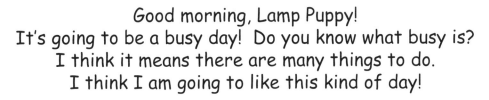

"Oh, Boyd-Friend... are you hungry?
It's time for breakfast!"

Breakfast... now there's a word I understand!
I'll be there faster than JUMPIN' JACKRABBITS!

"Good Boyd. Now that you have finished breakfast, let's go outside.
Sara will be coming soon. I am sure you will enjoy playing with her."

31

Look! Someone's coming! Who is it?
Hey, she's small like me!

"Hello, Sara! We've been expecting you.
This is curious little Boyd-Friend.
He's gentle, friendly and learns quickly.
Keep him on leash and give him time to know you.
Your mother and I will be right here while you play."

"Come on, Boyd-Friend!
Let's run down the fence line!"

"Well, it didn't take Sara long to make friends!"

JUMPIN' JACKRABBITS!
Do you like to play outdoors?
Would you like to be my running friend?
Do you have a bicycle?
I can run along side a bicycle while on leash!
I can even fetch toys if you have time to play.
Do you have food? I'm never late for snacks!
Whoa! Hugging was going to be my next question.
Thanks for that big squeeze!

Whew! I'm glad to go inside for a little rest.

Hey there, Washer Puppy! I was right.
It is a busy day and I have found another friend!
Her name is Sara. She is my running friend.
Can she run? Like JUMPIN' JACKRABBITS she can run!
Excuse me while I tell Lamp Puppy about her.

Hello again, Lamp Puppy!
I have a new friend, Sara.
Look! She's right here beside me.

"What do you see, Boyd-Friend?
Look everyone!
Boyd sees himself in this lamp!"

"He certainly does! He has a most unusual ability.
He can easily see things in reflective surfaces.
Dogs do not generally see things that way.
He is so funny when he admires himself in a shiny surface.
He prefers his image to that of toys. Imagine that!
And he likes being near people who speak gently.
You can even see him relax when he hears soft music.
Yet, he loves the outdoors and has a keen sense of smell.
At day's end he likes to curl at your feet on a soft cushion.
There is nothing not to like about this exceptional puppy.
But, of course, I believe all my dogs to be exceptional!"

Why don't you and Sara think about little Boyd-Friend this evening?
Caring for a pet is a big responsibility. Sometimes it seems overwhelming.
Think of all the things he will need... endless love in a permanent home to begin.
He'll need nutritious food that will allow him to grow and be healthy.
And daily exercise, regular baths and grooming will keep him fit and comfortable.
Be sure he always has a clean, soft bed and proper medical care.
You will also need to know the local laws for pet owners where you live.
So, there is a great deal of time and expense to consider before having a pet.
If you have no doubts about Boyd-Friend, stop by early tomorrow morning.
Breakfast is at eight o'clock and you are welcome to feed him.
Then we can talk more about what he needs to live a happy, healthy life.
Adopted dogs make wonderful, life-long companions when given proper care.
It doesn't take long before they become a member of the family and your best friend!

Sniff... sniff.
I wonder if I will ever see my running friend again...

"Good morning, Sara!
Did you come to feed a forever friend his breakfast?"

"Yes, Ma'am.
I played with Boyd-Friend and Lamp Puppy in my dreams last night.
And this morning I knew I wanted Boyd-Friend in my life forever!"

My running friend! You did come back! Oh me, oh my... you came for me!
YIPPIE-SKIPPIE and JUMPIN' JACKRABBITS!

"What a delightful life for Boyd-Friend...
at last, a forever friend AND a forever home!"

"I received an email from a friend last evening.
There is an abandoned puppy that needs love.
He's a mixed breed, found wandering near a lake and needing immediate care.
Like Boyd-Friend, he will be coming to live with me only for a short while.
Maybe someday you will have the pleasure of meeting Cowboy!"

"Isn't life good?"